# Kate Strike

*The girl who got it all*

*Saramah Hossain*

authorHOUSE®

AuthorHouse™
1663 Liberty Drive
Bloomington, IN 47403
www.authorhouse.com
Phone: 1 (800) 839-8640

Published by AuthorHouse   09/23/2016

ISBN: 978-1-5246-3964-8 (sc)
ISBN: 978-1-5246-3962-4 (hc)
ISBN: 978-1-5246-3963-1 (e)

Library of Congress Control Number: 2016915304

For my Mother,
Everything I write is to praise her, whom I owe forever.

# CONTENTS

*I smashed a bolt at the wall, out of my frustration, and created a small crack in it. I sighed, angry with myself......*

. . . . . . . . . . . . . . . . . . . . . . . . . . . . . . . . . . . . . . .

My name is Katelyn Strike but I'm better known as Kate. I am 14 years old and I go to ParceHollow Academy, a school for students who have Zodda's power. Speaking of Zodda, she is an ancient, powerful woman who at every child's birth gives a unique power to them. And once a child received that power, they keep it for eternity. Though Zodda is old, she still lives in the shadowy forests of Kregilia, the place where all of us humans live. She is known little at this time, but her legends carry on.

Speaking of power, mine is the power of lightening.

I love it ever so dearly. My whole family, even ancestors have lightening as their gift. I only have one father and no mother. She one day unexpectedly died without anyone knowing. Only some of my closest companions know. I am also the only child, so that makes my life harsher. I am usually a very quiet being, but when it comes to athletics, you should bring a doctor with you.

My school, ParceHollow Academy, has a very strict rule. Once you master your element Zodda has given you, you leave the place and begin to protect your part of land. A lot of my friends have left the academy and are somewhere off better. Only one hasn't left yet, Heather Sterling. She has the gift of the fire world, where she will soon guard the place at night and watch over everything that lurks by. She and I are on the same level and hopefully can leave together. My school has another strict biding; it divides us among two groups - Zodda and Thorcle, the two greatest people in the history of Kregilia. As you know Zodda, Thorcle was a powerful, yet selfish man to ever live. He and both Zodda give children the gift at birth but unlike Zodda, Thorcle gives influence and arrogance within the power, giving the child and his/her entire family, a miserable life. Thorcle lives till now but known just as equally as Zodda. The group of students in Zodda hates the students in Thorcle and Thorcle himself.

# ⚡ CHAPTER ONE ⚡

I smashed a bolt at the wall, out of my frustration, and created a small crack in it. I sighed, angry with myself for failing my 12th turn already.

"Kate! What have I told you about keeping your aiming straight?" Bozz said. He was one of my personal trainers at ParceHollow Academy. He was assigned to me because all of the other trainers failed to restrain me, but he hasn't. He is a very patient man, unlike any other I have ever seen. He is calm, but if you displease him too much, he enrages. But in this case I was trying and not purposely displeasing him. He was the only person that could calm me down when I was feeling unsecured.

"Coach Bozz, I am trying, okay! Can't you see how infuriating this is! If you were in my position you would under—." I stopped yelling and looked at his solid, dark skinned face. I realized I was raising my voice a little high and stopped. He was naturally like that, not really having any fun in life. I sighed and said, "I'm sorry Coach. I'll try to improve." I hung my head in depression. He sighed for a moment then replied, "Ok… I guess you had enough training and it's time for you to go." He gestured me out of the training simulator, and into a wide open corridor, inside the academy.

I glanced at every picture hung onto the wall. My dark brown hair swept side to side as I did. Every student that has graduated, his or her photo was strung onto the wall. I recognized many of them. Almost all of them were my friends and cousins. I admired all of the forces there, but soon grumbled at the fact that I was only Strike not having to achieve yet.

I followed Bozz at the end of the hallway until he led me into a small room; his office. The walls were crystal clear literally. His desk was at the middle of the room, with two other small chairs on each side of it. He offered me a seat across from him and seated himself. He spoke,

"Listen Kate, I know you have been training hard all day every day....but you're not seemed to improve." I bit the inside of my lip and looked down sideways. "So that's why the other school head-stress and I are planning to actually send you to a different training facility." My head shot straight up at the sound of it, but he continued. "I'm guessing you want to reject, but don't worry, we haven't quite gotten all the details yet, but for now, we just want your opinion."

For a moment I just sat there, dumbstruck. I couldn't believe that I was going to be leaving the academy. I couldn't do that, wouldn't. I had to go home every day to check on my father. He was extremely sick and I'd be worried about him. I swallowed hard and tried to sound as calm as I could and said, "The offer sounds helpful really but Coach Bozz, I have duties on my own hands. I can't just leave and go to a new training academy. I have to stay here and help my father out rather then moving out." Half of my speech came out calm but the other half came out in a desperation mode. But I continued anyways. "Look, I know that you and I are both really desperate to master my element.

You have trained me for almost 2 years now. I think you are just as eager as I am. And don't get me wrong Coach Bozz. I really want to graduate and live free, but that's not going to happen so easily when my only true family is sick at home. I'm sorry, but I don't think I'm ready for now. When my father revives, I'll try to think it over, for sure." Bozz looked at me for a moment in a blank expression. I couldn't really tell what he was thinking about but suddenly he smiled and chuckled a little. "You know, I admire how loyal you are to your loved ones. You know one of my old friends back in the day used to train your father. You and your father have a lot in common. I find it amusing though," he said smiling. I smiled too but then soon stopped when he brought up the next part. "Kate, you do know that your father's suffering a really hard disease, right?" I nodded bitterly. "It would take him a long while to heal, right?" he asked and I nodded again. "So you are aware that you have to send your father to Kregilian's personal doctor, right?" he asked but this time I didn't nod nor say anything.

After a long moment I spoke, "He hates us, doesn't he?" I asked so coldly that it nearly made any body quiver. "Kate –," Bozz started, but I cut him off. "He would never do anything to help us, not ever. Not even if my father or I, or whoever I'm related to is almost about to die, he still would lough bitterly and decline, wouldn't he?" I asked again and again coldly. Bozz looked at me for a moment before answering, "Ah…Kate, he has changed. Dr. Bolin isn't a bad man anymore. I know some rumors say that he was the one who started the Kregilian war that came upon us 10 years ago, but he did really regret doing it sometime later. And believe me Kate, he –." I cut him off again before he finished.

"He is a terrible man. Coach Bozz, I don't think you understand what I really feel about Dr. Bolin. We all know that he regretted about starting that war 10 years ago, but I'm the only one to remember what he did to my mother. They used to work together at a lab as partners, and he poisoned her a little while later. After that, my mother was ill for many months before I was born. She suffered until I was 11 years old and soon....disappeared without anyone knowing." I shook my head with anger and instead said.

"Never mind, it doesn't really matter what had happened and what is going to happen. I just want to get my mind clear right now. So if you don't mind Coach Bozz, I would really like it if you were to train me again. Just for fun and practice. And I'll promise you this. I promise that I'll......I'll think about the whole going to train somewhere else thing, and give you an answer very soon."

"Alright Kate, you can train now, but I'm warning you. You can't fail me again, understand?" Bozz said harshly that my face fell. Then suddenly Bozz laughed at my reaction and said, "Just kidding Kate! Wow, you are easy to mess with!" I flushed so red you could literally see my blood sizzling out of me. I laughed along with him and then we walked back to the huge, open arena where the training was.

I shot one grin back over my shoulder to Bozz, as I picked up my bow and struck a bolt at the last remaining target. For the first time in 2 weeks, I got it and smiled.

# ⚡ CHAPTER TWO ⚡

The outside world was dark, as the first smallest dim of light began to shine through the horizon.

It was really early in the morning and I sprang out of bed and already started to get ready for school. Today was an important day because one of the Zodda's teachers is going to teach us a very skillful and dangerous technique at training today. Ms. Eva, the teacher said that it was going to be a very dangerous move so we all had to wear something secured. And so I found one.

It was a skin tight black short sleeved shirt with a thin vest covering the collar. It also had a dark brown belt to go around with it. I also wore some matching skin tight black jeans too that seemed perfect with the shirt. I put my hair in a side brand on my shoulders with a few strands covering my right eye. Then I looked into a mirror and I froze right there on that spot. I looked just like my mother when she was my age. I stared at my reflection for a very long time and admired the fact that I look just like my mother......before I actually saw her in the mirror. I gasped and jerked back. Though I saw her only for a split second, the image frightened me. I had so many rare photos of her in the house. My father has loved her as equally as I did, and thought it was a tragic to have her gone, so he hide, maybe threw out, all of her photos with her and with us. Even when he took all the photos, I still managed to keep some and hide it in my room. My father doesn't know and won't ever. I'll make sure of it.

My father and I had gotten into a lot of arguments lately, and it's not seemed to get any better. Though he is sick, he can still keep his ground no matter what the situation was. I truly enjoy my time being alive with everything in life, but having the stress with my training and father was not fun at all.

I sighed and rubbed my forehead from not exploding. I still had a few minutes before the big bell rang from ParceHollow Academy and indicated us that it was time to leave for training. I didn't have anything to do so I sat on my bed, before I changed my mind into standing on the bed. As I stood on the bed, I unwrapped a pair of leather folding out from on top of the ceiling that covered it. As I took out the leather, it uncovered a small brown box. I brought it down and opened it up.

Inside it was many small photos of my parents and me together. It also had a note written from my mother on the right before she died. It was crumply, but I kept it anyways. I then fumbled about through the box, until I found a rectangular shaped photo of my mom single. She was standing up high with broad shoulders with a mischievous expression on her face. My mother was bit of a trouble maker back then. I grinned at the thought of her pranking on one of her teachers at school. Unlike me, she had the guts to do it.

My mother had dark green emerald eyes that flashed her true self. She had on smirk and had light brown flowing hair. She was wearing almost one of the exact outfits that I was wearing right now. I was amazed at all the similarities we shared. I was about to go through more pictures, but the bell rang and it was time for me to go. I packed up everything, put it all back, went downstairs, kissed my father goodbye-regretting the moment when I got mad at him--, and soon ran off to the academy. By now, the dim light that was there before burst into a huge bright ray warming up the land of Kregilia.

At somewhat point, I surprisingly arrived earlier than usual. The arena was empty, just barely filled with a few students whom I presume, are here for Ms. Eva's training today. I glanced around the arena, trying to find Heather. I spotted her just around the corner of the arena where the long tables filled with equipment and gadgets were. I was about to go walk up to her, but then an evil idea crossed my mind. I was going to go run up to her and jump on her shoulders which could easily give her a heart attack, considering the fact that she was a person who got scared very easily.

I glanced around the arena once to make sure some students were watching, as I ran for a head start approaching her and jumped onto her shoulders, snickering like crazy. The instant I touched her, she screamed so loud that it probably shattered the ears of the nearby birds that were flying above and dropped a piece of cloth she had in her hand.

I laughed so hard that my sides hurt. Her face turned beat-red with embarrassment which made me laugh even more. Heather sighed, "Hahaha.....very funny Kate! It's seemed like the only interest you have these days is scaring the life out of me." I stopped laughing but tried to contain again from not happening at Heather's annoyance. As an apology, I gently picked up the cloth that she was holding and handed it to her. "Look Heath," I said using her nickname, "I am sorry. I thought it would just be funny to see your perplexed face once I scare you. And yeah, maybe you're right that the only interest I had recently is just scaring you, but that help keeping all the stress going on in my head vanish." Suddenly her smile disappeared as mine. "You're doing extra training with Bozz aren't you Kate?" she asked seriously. I heaved out a breath and replied, "Yeah I just – Heather why am I not succeeding my powers quick enough?" Heather looked at me for a second before answering. "Look Kate, it's okay. I mean, I too am getting impatient of my situation, but – at least you are moving forward." I interrupted her, "I was stuck at one position for almost 2 years, Heath. I'm not achieving anything and when I do, its take such a long time just to get it right." "Kate, all I can say to you now and always, is just be patient, okay. I promise things will work out eventually for you and me. Just you wait and see", said orange-haired girl. I couldn't do anything but appreciate her encouragement, and smile slightly. She returned the smile only for moment, before a very high pitched whistle shot out, penetrating the air around it. I knew that whistle meant it was time to start training.

"Alright everyone takes your position!" said Ms. Eva. Ms. Eva was a very calm and athletic person. She has a strong heart and is willing than ever to accomplish us. I looked so much up to her. She had to be around her mid 40's hinting it because of her short, beautifully white wavy hair that covered one of her eyes. She has treated all of the students with extreme care. She almost felt like a mother to me. I would usually spend most of my free times with her, getting advice and sharing stories with each other. But now was not the time to share stories.

# ⚡ CHAPTER THREE ⚡

Every single student – even their limbs obeyed Ms. Eva right away. We were very discipline here in ParceHollow Academy. No one mistrusted, misjudged, nor disobeyed anyone here. We were like one very powerful army standing together in force, ready to fight! But fight what?

"Alright now that you are all in base position, I want you to listen very carefully at what you're about to hear and see," said Ms. Eva. She grabbed a small metal solid brick from her table, and placed it squarely on the ground. Then she stepped a few inches back and turned left to face at our direction. She spoke, "Okay.......now one by one, I want you to come up here and try to cast a portal, ok? Then, I want you to step inside of it slowly and carefully and see what holds before you. But be careful, it can be very, very, dangerous. That's why I've asked you all to wear protective gear. Now....do I make myself clear?" "Yes, Ms. Miss," we all said. Ms. Eva grinned and told the first person in line to step up. Her name is Cyd Shurk. She has black slick hair that falls to her back, and she is somewhat a very scared person. Everyone can tell because of her strict actions and face that always seemed to be glued together so we can't really tell what she is feeling. And like everyone else, she had gear that was covering every inch of her body. Only her elbow, down part was showing. She began to make her portal.

Everyone here at the academy had to learn to make portal from when they were very young. It is unusual for all of us to have one thing in common. We rarely ever use it; only in critical and training moments.

Cyd placed her hands in a circular motion and light blue began to sputter her fingers. Cyd moved her hands harder and faster this time, creating a larger opening. Cyd exhaled out jerkily. Portals were very tricky to do. After a while, Ms. Eva came to her side and placed one hand on her shoulder, trying to calm and instruct her. "Ok Cyd. Now what I want you to do is, slowly place your portal on top of the brick, okay?" Ms. Eva asked. Cyd nodded hesitantly. Her portal becomes very large now, almost taking half of her body. A sweat trickled down her left forehead.

Cyd carefully pushed her portal on the brick but continued casting since it wasn't big enough. After some moments, Ms. Eva whispered into her ear, "Alright Cyd, that's enough." Relieved Cyd smiled shortly and stopped casting. She was panting quietly but smirked at what she accomplished. Her portal was a large blue lit, oval shaped passageway that led ….. Who knows where? We all had no idea what the portals desire or mean. The type that we used, were for transportation from one area to another. But Cyd's portal looked kind of different today.

Suddenly, out of nowhere, the metal brick changed color from silver to now a deep red. It was also sizzling for some reason. "Today, I wanted to show you all a skill that is called Lumination Devition. This work of art is very tremendous to do. This lesson isn't going to teach you anything powerful OR athletic but will teach you moderation and deviation," Ms. Eva said. "As you can see here, the brick seemingly changed colors. This is based on how it feels about the person's portal and the person him or herself. We humans haven't discovered all the colors and its options yet, but somewhat you will be learned some here right now." And with that, Ms. Eva held up one finger and a light orange string of light passed through her finger and then around the portal. Just then the portal began to make some wind noises and whispering something no one can really catch. Cyd's portal was wanting her to step inside.

Ms. Eva said in Cyd's ear, "Alright Cyd. Now all I'm going to ask for you to do is slowly walk inside your portal, okay?" Cyd looked at Ms. Eva one last time and nodded. Then she looked back at us and gulped. She started moving forward until she was centimeters away. She held out one hand to touch it and go in, but immediately as she did, she screamed and jumped back. Cyd glanced at Ms. Eva who spoken, "Yes my dear students, this technique will hurt a lot and might even get the chance to kill you. That's why you all have protective gear on, am I right?" Ms. Eva nodded and gave a reassuring smile at Cyd, who was clutching her hand out of agony. She stammered and tried again, this time with narrowed eyes. I kind of chuckled at her brave contempt.

Cyd inhaled and then put her legs and arms inside the portal. She screamed even harder this time but didn't stop. She screamed until her whole body went through the portal. After she went in, the second she did, the entire portal disappeared in a flash. I jerked my neck, clearly shocked. I have never seen a portal vanish like that and so suddenly. Well maybe that was the whole point of which this training is based on, right?

Cyd didn't return in quite some time now. I glanced over at Heather in concern. She had the same expression. I glanced back to where the portal used to be and saw nothing there, only the red brick which still seems to sizzling a little. Then I glanced back at Ms. Eva. She had on a plain face that didn't really give away anything, but her eyes explained it all. She was concerned but more scared. I looked at the ground then back to the 11 lined up students who were pale with confusion. I was starting to worry.

Just some more time later, we all heard a huge wisp sound and saw the portal return. Only this time it wasn't blue, it was pitch black. That kind of frightened me to the bones. After some more moments later, we all heard a shriek coming from inside the portal. I could just make out with Cyd's feet and face but nothing else for now. Slowly emerging, Cyd appeared fully at the entrance. She looked normal, until I noticed her now torn up gear, bare arms that were slightly burnt, and a large scratch at her right arm. The students and I were beyond terrified now. When Cyd finally walked a few inches away from her portal, she let out a whimper and collapsed on the ground on her back. All of the students, even Ms. Eva came rushing at Cyd's side. I managed to get beside her. I looked at her face and saw that she had also cut a thin line on her left cheek. It wasn't bleeding but it was red and slightly swollen. I started to breathe rapidly as her eyes started to get heavy and shut down. A girl beside me yelped and darted to look at Ms. Eva, who is by now, shaking. "I – I don't understand, I mean I casted a spell to protect her from harm, but ---," she stammered out. I quickly checked her pulse. Thank Goodness that she was still breathing.

Ms. Eva quickly ran inside the academy's corridor and came back shortly with two white uniformed doctors. She told them about the situation and they quickly lunged Cyd on their shoulders and placed one arm around her back and front from not letting her fall. Eventually they only reached a few spaces forward before they couldn't carry her anymore. Cyd, again, crashed on the ground. Finally one of the doctors volunteered to carry her to the hospital wing at ParceHollow.

No one really spoke after that. No sound came out of anywhere. No emotion sprung out of anything, just the yelling commotion that going inside our bodies. Ms. Eva looked stunned and didn't expect this to happen. None of us did.

# ⚡ CHAPTER FOUR ⚡

It has been almost a day since the incident with Cyd and the portal. Everyone was still confused and scared at what we all witnessed. Ms. Eva was sure to cast a protective spell for Cyd, but it didn't seem to do its trick.

It was the time of the year where all of us at ParceHollow Academy prepare ourselves for the upcoming tournament we had. It was very exciting and I have only experienced it once so I was happy to do it again.

I walked downstairs to the kitchen and got a small snack because I got hungry. I didn't really bother to go to training early today because there wasn't much going on right now. The head teachers at ParceHollow are just organizing the battle arena for our tournament and announced that the students could come and train for fun, if they wanted.

I finished eating and went back upstairs to my father's room. I stood outside his door for a moment and inhaled slowly before walking in. When I did, I saw him lying in his bed sleeping. Well maybe he was half awake because the moment I stepped in, he glanced at my direction, smiling. I knelt beside his bed and looked up at him returning the smile. "Good morning, Daddy," I spoke quietly. He cleared his throat and then replied hoarsely, "Good morning Kate. Have you slept well?" "Yes, I have Daddy," I said. "Daddy I know I already asked you this some time, but when are you going to get better?" I sort of plead at that last part.

He sighed and then spoke, "You know I don't know, Kate. I'm trying my best to find the right hospital, but none of them seems to be working. They don't what kind of illness I have, unfortunately. It is something they don't understand and neither ever we will."

We looked at each other for a moment before I said, "But I do understand one thing.....Mother died and

I can't have you gone too, Daddy." I can't help myself but bite my lip from not crying.

There was a moment of silence after I stated this comment. I breathed warily, afraid I might have said something wrong. But after a while, my father took a hold of my hand and said in reassuring voice, "I am never going to leave you Kate. Not ever. You believe that, okay." By now, I had started shaking a little. I gripped my father's hand tighter and hoped that things will soon get better. I know they will.

It has been some time now, and the sun was now peaking over Kregilia and brightly shining down at the land. It had to be around noon by now and I decided that I would just go to the academy to get some fresh air. And so I changed my clothes and instead ware a pale, dark blue shirt with some black pants. I also tied my hair into my everyday braids with a few strands coming out, and headed outdoors. I didn't immediately go over to the academy. I first went through a nearby forest that was close to the arena. The forest wasn't exactly that huge, but it was very beautiful when the sun beamed on it. The tall green trees were gently shifting side-by-side at the cold breeze that passed by. I closed my eyes for a moment, a moment, and inhaled the sweet scent that was, not far, coming from a close by stream that was up ahead. I grinned and decided to go there too.

When I reached the slow moving stream that was surrounded by some small birds and squirrels, I carefully dipped my feet inside. I normally from time-to-time do this often when I feel bored and just want to clear my mind off things and just relax. The cold water smoothed my legs and I sighed, why can't life be like this every day; so calm and peaceful. Suddenly the burden thought about me moving to a new training system, washed through me. I frowned slightly at the thought of it why did I have to move? Why can't I just stay here at ParceHollow and continue here? Well, even if I were to, I still couldn't accomplish anything. It just felt so difficult and confusing all at once. I shook my head grumpily and took my legs out of the water. I then found a close by tree and leaned against the base of it. I spread out my feet to let them dry in the sun. Alarmingly, my eyes started to feel heavy and were dropping. Of course they would. Through all of this comfort and the nature around me, I couldn't help but just let my body fall into an ocean of sleep.

I wasn't aware of how much time had gone by and woke up with an alarming start as I saw a face in front of me. "Hello? Are you alright?" the sudden face piped out. I quickly jerked my head back and stood up. I turned to the side and saw the face that spoke. He looked to be around a few years older than me, though he didn't seem like it. He had dark blonde shaggy hair that covered most of his eyes and had a creamy face, which seems to be grinning. He probably still amused at my reaction. He also had on a white t-shirt that seems to be kind of torn at the bottom. He had on some pants that reached his ankles. I couldn't help but lough a little. It was rude, so I stopped and asked "Um, what is your name?" He didn't answer right away and cockily stared at the ground. When he looked puzzled at first but then replied, clearly embarrassed, "Oh uh, sorry. Well my name is Siffrin Lyrimon. What is yours?"

"Kate Strike," I replied eyeing him curiously, but then shook it off. "Anyway, what are you doing here?" Siffrin asked me. "I think the better question is what happened to your shirt?" I smirked stupidly. He looked down at his clothes and replied smiling, "Oh, you know, I was just climbing one of these trees and fell down somehow." I nodded and started to turn but he added, "Wait! You haven't answered my question yet." I looked at him like he was crazy, but he just shrugged innocently. I sighed and replied, "Well I walked from home to this nearby forest and you know, just taking a stroll, I guess. And...wait, why should I be even telling you this in the first place? He looked at me for a second before laughing. He calmed down and said, "Who ever told you that you had to answer me?" I narrowed my eyes at him and said, "But you're the one who asked me first!" "And you listened!" Siffrin chuckled. My mouth gaped opened. How could he have tricked me? I grumbled and shook my head heading back, not in the mood.

He called after me, "Wait, Kate! I'm sorry! I didn't mean to-." When he noticed that I wasn't turning back he raced after me and grabbed my wrist. I spun around and again, narrowed my eyes at him. I let go of his grasps and shook my head, "Look, Siffrin, I know that you were just messing around with me, but honestly I have to get going. I need to go, do some training at the academy. I intended to say something else, but he spoke first. "Wait, you go to the academy? You mean ParceHollow Academy?" I stood there for a moment and then nodded. "Oh cool. I graduated from that place about 2 months ago. It's fun there right?" I nodded but deep inside it really wasn't. "So, what ability do you have?" he asked. I replied "I have the power of lightening or bolts – that I got from Zodda. How about you?" "Mine is the ability to use and materialize spells and potions. I know it sounds kind of silly." I shook my head, "No it doesn't….well maybe a little." He cocked on eyebrow. I chuckled, "okay, I'm kidding, may be not that much."

After a moment he looked like he has seen a ghost and his face turned green. I looked puzzled and asked, "What's wrong?" He stumbled back, but then managed to spill out, "My mother strictly told me to come home without getting my new shirt ruined. And if I did she'd kill me!" He paced around rapidly before finally saying, "Okay, well, I guess I'll see you later, Kate." He quickly ran away before I could have replied. But either way, I just stood there laughing.

# ⚡ CHAPTER FIVE ⚡

When I reached the academy it was almost dark. The sky seemed to have turned purple and the star started to emerge. So I quickly got inside and breathed out.

After a moment not too soon, Heather came up to me. "Hey Kate," said quietly. "Um, hey Heath. What's up? You look down," I replied noticing her pale face. She shook her head and grabbed me by the wrist and led me to the hospital wing. On the way, I kept on asking where she was taking me, but gave up at some point.

When we reached at the door, not going in yet, Heather held my shoulders firmly and said, "Kate, it's terrible, Cyd is in very bad condition. I – you know what, never mind. It's better if I show you." I was surprised she said that all in one breathe, but got even more surprised when I stepped inside the hospital wing.

Some students were bunched around a bed that I couldn't properly make out, but did when I reached there. I gasped at what I saw. Others closed their eyes or looked away. Heather tightened her grip on my arm. Cyd was lying on the bed, half alive half dead. Her scars from the training day had now grew twice as swollen and her face looked flushed.

I gently started stroking on her right hand that was bit red. But decided to hold it warmly on mine. Cyd made a small whimper, then a bigger one. Until finally, some words came out in a hushed whisper, "Kate...... hi..." I quickly shushed her and said, "Shh...Cyd. You need your strength to live. Don't worry. We're all here. Just relax. You would be doing me a great favor." Cyd then slightly smiled and I smiled back. Before long, two nurses came in the hospital wing and rushed us all out of Cyd's bed. We quietly said our goodbyes before going to the arena for some training.

Heather and I were assigned as partners and geared up. All the students were working as pairs and collected their weapons from a nearby table.

When we finished, Heather and I went to the center of the arena and started. Heather was the one to aim and I would be the one to back it. This was called Defending Divination. I myself and all the other students here knew this very well. So it was easy at first. But as you increase your ease of blocking, the aimer will increase their speed of shooting. Most of the time I was the aimer but now I instead chose to be defender.

As we began, I created a shield vortex and held it up to my chest, while Heather was lighting fire ball in her right hand. You might think it's easy but we were actually 20 feet apart! So it is definitely not easy for the both of us.

"Ready?" Heather called out to me. I shouted back in response. Heather stepped a few feet back and then came running at full speed and threw her fire ball. I instantly located where it was going and dodged it by hitting my shield in front of my head. As soon as it hit, the fire ball crimpled under my feet and heated down. Heather held up thumbs up and I knew she was congratulating me, but then soon her friendly smile vanished and replaced it with a wicked smirk. I clearly noted that meant that she was going to go harder this time and I smirked back, ready.

Just then Heather created two fireballs and sent them flying along with an extra one. I perfectly blocked all three and called out to her, "Uh come on, Heath. Give me a harder shot!" Heather sighed and shoot her head, feeling pity at what I just demanded. Without a warning, Heather now randomly sent a lot of fire balls in my direction. There were so many that I couldn't locate all of them so just did what came to me. I did some backward flips and dodged four balls. Then I did front flips and dodged five balls. Then I did sideway flip but managed to get two balls. I was exhausted and so was Heather but we needed this type of training for the upcoming tournament that was, not too long, to come.

Heather and I went on like this for about two hours before I held up a hand. Heather saw and cooled down the ball that she was just creating. I only managed to breathe out, "Wait……" before I collapsed and sat down crossed leg. Heather rolled her eyes, laughed and jogged up to meet me. She, too, sat on the arena's floor facing me. After a while of catching her breathe she asked, teasingly, "Seriously, Kate? You're tired already? Psh, soon enough you'd have to join the senior knitting club." I stuck out my tongue at her and we joked all afternoon.

Finally I said, "You know the Annual ParceHollow Tournament is coming up." "I know" Heather replied, not taking this seriously. I sighed and tried again, "Heather, what have you been practicing for?" Now this captured her attention. She said, "Well, you know how much I love Fire Acrobats. Half of me comes from the Fire lands." "Oh, so is that why your hair is flaming?" I joked. Heather rolled her eyes and continued. "So I decided to join up at that team." "And how long have you been practicing?" I asked. Heather thought for a moment before replying, "For about two weeks." I nodded.

"So how about you, Kate? What are you practicing for?" Heather asked. "Royal Archery." She snorted and I cocked an eyebrow. "What?" Heather gathered herself up after a moment and said, "It's just that, you've been into that for so long and couldn't accomplish anything." I narrowed my eyes and punched her arm playfully and said, "Yeah right. As if you could do any better!" Heather chuckled and said more quietly this time, "We'll just see." "Yes we will," I whispered back.

# ⚡ CHAPTER SIX ⚡

The sun was dimly gleaming on my window as I fluttered my eyes, starting the day with an excited feeling inside more.

Today was the day of the tournament, and I was ready than ever. I stupidly stumbled out of my bed and groaned in annoyance. I quickly sat up and looked at the time. It was by now very early dawn as I headed for the shower. When I came back I brushed my slick dark hair and chose what to wear. As I was rummaging through my closet, I decided to wear something no one has seen me in before. Usually all the students come in the same training outfit every day, so it was easy to pick something out.

But I found no luck. I didn't really have that many options as I looked and finally gave up. Since it was still a bit early, I went ahead to check on my dad to see if he could help me. As I quietly entered his room which was at the end of the hallway, I saw him already up and sitting at his desk. He heard my footsteps and slowly turn to face me. "Good morning, Kate. Are you ready for the tournament?" he asked then slightly coughed. I shrugged and replied, "Well, not really. Since today is the tournament and the 200th anniversary of it, I wanted to wear something different and.......special."

My father looked at me for a moment then looked at his closet that was beside his desk. He thought for a second of hesitation before shrugging it off. "Don't worry, Kate. I think I might have something.....special, for you to wear," he said. Then he smiled and walked over to the closet and opened it. It was filled with some of his clothing and some boxes with files in them. But he took out something from behind those boxes and revealed a black package that was neatly wrapped.

"This box contained your mother's first and ever tournament outfit. I have kept it for some time because your mother wanted you to wear it someday. It might not be extraordinary, but it means something to us. I hope you like it," my father said. I stared at the box for a moment then carefully took a hold of it.

It wasn't very heavy, but I'm sure the confidence that my mother had when she wore this outfit weighed more than anything you could imagine. I smiled, hoping that when I wear it I might get the same feeling. I looked up to face my father and said, "Thank you, Daddy. I'll make sure to make you….and Mom happy. I promise." "Oh, we know you'll do just fine, Kate. Just try your best and have fun." I hugged my father, and then left his room, feeling like a courageous, fierce lion.

When I entered my room I placed the package on the bed and gently opened it. When I removed the cover, it revealed another white cloth. Underneath that, laid the real prize.

I carefully lifted up the beautifully, silk woven dress -which is how it looked like – and stared at it in owe. It was black mixed with a little bit of silver that enclosed like a circle around the neck. Made sense, because it had no sleeves. It also had the same pattern running down the whole piece of cloth. The pants were attached to the top so it was all one piece. I grinned and put it on.

After I put it on, I faced the mirror that was beside my drawer. I didn't realize so clearly before, but the silver had small piece of white jams on it. It felt amazing, really. I couldn't think that this would still fit me after all these years. But either way, I was extremely happy.

I opened up one of the drawers and brought out two, black matching gloves. I patched it around my fingers then started working on my hair. I decided to put it back in a bun-since my hair might fall into my eyes – but kept out some strings of hair to fall to the side. I finished dressing and outside looked like a sunny day. The last thing I needed was my bow and arrows. I picked it out from my chest that contained some of my other training gadgets and went downstairs to eat. I quickly ate small bread and some cheese and milk and braced myself for what will behold me today and forever as I walked into the outdoor sunshine.

My mind literally blown off when I arrived at ParceHollow. They have expanded the academy by letting in some more grounds. It also had colorful banners hanging from the side of the academy's top, which was completely open so you could see the sky. I saw hundreds of students from all parts of training areas in Kregilia warming up for the tournament. But at the far end corner, I saw my school district. There were the teams Zodda and Thorcle both aggressively working out. Just then I spotted Heather at the simulator table, writing something down. I was about to go walk up to her, but suddenly heard a voice from beside me that startled me. "Hey. You must be Kate, right?" I recognized that voice from the woods. It was Siffrin. I replied, "Yep, that's me."

Siffrin looked awfully different today. Last time I saw him, his blonde hair was covering his eyes, but right now he instead had his hair slicked back that pumped out a little at the top, which made two strands fall on his forehead. He also wore a gray t-shirt that was covered by a white jacket. And to go with that, he had on some black tight jeans. I nearly choked out laughing at his major difference but remained cool.

"Oh, so you must be Siffrin. Huh, didn't really catch you fast enough through the different clothing." He slightly frowned and said, "My mom forced me to wear this. This is nothing like me. I am like the opposite." Seemed about right. "So, anyway, what are you doing here?" I asked. "Came to see the ParceHollow tournament. I've been in this thing for four years now. Been amazing really." "I see," I said. After a moment he added, "So what have been training for?" "Royal Archery," I stated firmly. He nodded before saying, "Well, I guess you should go practice, I guess. I mean tournament is starting in less than an hour."

A horrified shock ran through my body as I forgot that we had to practice. "Oh, right!" I totally forgot. Okay, um, I guess I'll see you later then?" I said. "Um, I guess you will," he said, smiling. I smiled back before rapidly running over to the Royal Archery Simulator table to catch up on my team and start practicing. But before I did I bumped into Heather. We collided but luckily didn't fall down. "Woah, Kate! Slow down,"

Heather said. "Oops! Sorry, Heather," I said. "Hey, have you seen –," I started to say but stopped when I saw what she was wearing. "Have you seen what...?" Heather was saying before she, apparently looked at me in owe. She looked absolutely beautiful! I couldn't even tell between the now Heather and the before Heather. She had her orange hair lying loose around her back with some gold bits on one side of her face, creating a fire symbol. But it was the outfit that amazed me. She wore a light brown and golden tank top, which similar to mine, enclosed around the neck. She also wore a pair of golden and light brown tights since she was going to be doing acrobats. We both smiled each other and wanted to complement one another, but that was when, Sr. Anders, our tournament organizer, blew a whistle and called us to gather around.

# ⚡ CHAPTER SEVEN ⚡

I looked from the staff benches to see the first from go off to battle. Sr. Anders led us behind a room that was connected to the arena, where we all had to sit and wait for our teams to be called upon the field, and talk to us about the tournament rules.

The room that we were in was pretty large and filled with a lot of steel benches that we sat on. Each team had their own serial number so we knew when to go out. My team's number was 5 and Heather's was 4. Each team has ten members on both sides. Thorcle and Zodda had a total of 20 teams to go through so it will be a long tournament. But we waited.

The first team to out was Grand Casting from Zodda and then it was followed by Thorcle. Both these teams had to try to cast 100 different spells and potions in less than 30 minutes. After that, they had to compete with each other and see whose spell was stronger. I am pretty sure when Siffrin was back in ParceHollow he competed in this round and is now tentatively watching. Grad Casting took about 20 minutes until both teams were finished. Then one-by-one, each player from their teams started casting. Now this went on for about an hour before we all noticed team Thorcle was leading. I made a movement in my jaw and kept watching.

Finally, team Thorcle had the strongest spell and defeated team Zodda. And the mic went on and announced the winner: "And the winner of Grad Casting is, Thorcle!" A chorus of half boos and half cheers filled the arena. Then the two were escorted back to a different room. After that the next team came up.

This event was called Vortex Simulation. It's where you had to defend yourselves with your very own vortex shield and huge cannon will shoot out fire and electrified balls. How you win this is by seeing who doesn't get hit. The team with the most members win. And so it began.

This event took much longer than Grad Casting did and was very exciting. Both these teams were extremely good at this. But in Zodda there was a personal best player and his name was Nev Curtling. He had won four ParceHollow Annual Tournaments at Vortex Simulation so we all knew him very well. There were two members left in each team and Nev was one of them. At last, one member from Thorcle got shot and another until there was no more. Team Zodda has won. "And the Vortex Simulation winner is, Zodda!" A very loud chorus of cheers came from the audience, and Nev stuck out his tongue and he and the other members did a victory salute and left the arena field. At least we weren't falling behind.

The third event came and it was called Extreme Medieval. This was honestly one of my favorite events to watch as it is very dangerous and fun. In this, you had to fly on this hover board called Zion and try to knock off one of the other player's balance. It was dangerous because the players had to fly out of the arena and fly someplace else. But we had large digital screens that would track to where they were going. Cyd was a very good player in this round and it made me sad to see her not competing here. But I pushed those thoughts away and focused on what was happening now.

Also in this event there would have to be a referee coach flying with the players to count each one as it fell of its balance. And because of that there would have to be a monitor to watch you in case anything happens. The official referee blew the whistle and the players flew off.

Everyone watched half of the event until we had to watch the large screens because the teams flew off somewhere out of reach. I smiled as I watched the students flying so high up in the sky. But then slightly frowned as two Zodda players falling off.

This event was right handedly very terrifying. I could tell because the audience made a lot of worried sounds when one fell off its Zion. The teams weren't as far as I expected. Just a few miles away from the arena around the nearby close hills and Kregilia's council towers. They were like medium sized buildings that looked like houses but more thinner. As I was looking at the screen, I completely forgot about the event. Just as I did, I saw a young girl falling off her Zion but managed to hold on the edge of it with a hand.

The arena filled with hushed whispers as they watched. The young girl, I couldn't recognize, looked pale. Even more than her dark blonde hair. After some time later she struggled for falling, but then she grabbed another's hand and climbed back up again. As she did the arena cooled down again and cheered. The girl gave one last grin speeding off again. She looked a lot like Siffrin if you compare them closely. They both had the same amused grin when they smile, and both have the same color of blonde hair. Could this young girl possibly be Siffrin's sister? I looked over to the crowd of people and found Siffrin smiling big at the girl's accomplishment. Maybe she could be. But I had to find that out later as the tournament was on, and kept on going.

Eventually, team Thorcle won and we were all pretty disappointed. But then a smirk flew over Heather's face because it was her team's turn to compete. She and her team stood up and were about to leave, but before that Heather gave me a smile and I gave back a wink as they emerged onto the arena, very ready to compete.

# ⚡ CHAPTER EIGHT ⚡

The large loops that were decorated with fire, outfit the entire arena. The fire was blistering before my eyes as I looked at it. I was very excited and couldn't wait to see Heather's performance. I knew she would be too.

Team Thorcle and Zodda were lined up horizontally and both faced the massive fired loops. They were blazing. I could only imagine how hot it would be for the players in the field. They must be boiling. An official referee walked up to the front of the two teams, checked if they were ready – of course they are ready, why wouldn't they be-, and blew the whistle for the event to start.

How this worked out is that one player from each team will do as many stunts through the loops and then the next loops. This will go on until all pairs are finished and see which team did more impressive moves. I squinted my eyes enough to see who Heather was teamed up with. I couldn't get a clear shot but I just made it out enough to see that it was a boy. A few years older assume. He had kind of long black hair that edged on his forehead. He was also kind of skinny but at the same time, not too lanky. He was wearing a dark orange, skin tight tank top, with some black jeans that looked reasonable to play with. Heather had her opponent as a guy. Well this was going to be interesting.

The match started off with two males competitors. The first one from Thorcle's team went and did some jaw-dropping moves. He twisted so accurately around the fired loops that I thought he almost touched them. But he didn't. On his final move he did a side twisting back flip and landed. Maybe a little shaky but he managed to balance it off. The boy brushed a hand through his hair to wipe some sweat off and then walked back to the side of the arena where he sat on a bench, on the call of the referee. Now it was the next player's turn.

His name is Zayn Devons. I knew him because we used to do some training together back in the day. We didn't talk much or socialize. Just some average greetings or so.

Before Zayn went, he closed his eyes for only a second, and then rapidly speed off through the loops. His moves were just as impressive as his opponents were. He quickly jumped, ducked, twisted, and dodged all the fired loops before coming in for a landing. He did a few flips before spinning into the air and landed on one knee. He looked up and gave one smirk back to his opponent and then sat on the side of the arena on a different bench.

I squinted my eyes before gasping, realizing that Heather was next. I smiled at her but she probably couldn't see me. She and her opponent, whose name I know, is Pirie Brewer, lined up side-by-side, five feet across from each other, stared at the obstacle that lay in front of them. There were almost a dozen of fired loops and in between them, there were some hand bars that you could grab onto and swing yourself up high if you wanted. I shuddered to myself, thinking how this is even possible to do. I could never had done it that's for sure. I focused back on Heather, trying to be focused and not zoning out again.

Pirie went first. He rolled his head back on his shoulders a few times, before launching off. He first grabbed onto a high bar and flipped through the air and past the loop. He did the same thing for the next and the next. His ideas may be the same but he was extremely fast at it, you could literally see a blur sometimes. For his last three remaining loops, he nearly got burnt on his second one, and that kind of scared me. But they were all professionally trained students and knew what they were doing. And because of that his landing was fluent and balanced and he did very well.

There was some clapping afterwards and Pirie went to sit down on the bench. I shifted where I was sitting and now it was Heather's turn. I eyed her very carefully, hoping that I didn't miss anything, and wished her luck.

Heather slowly approached forward and took a long, nice breath. She then brushed a few strands of her hair out of her face before, not too soon, sprang off. I noticed how her grip on the bars were very firm and strong. She did not once hesitate to do any risk and kept going. Some of her moves were actually a bit too scary and crowed were whispering. One of her moves that got me hooked on the edge was when she tried to jump through the fired hoop to the next without holding the bars! I honestly thought she wouldn't be able to do it, at that moment I learnt to never think twice about Heather. That girl really has got the moves.

On the last four hoops that were remaining, she did a sideway flip and an extra front flip, which was extremely hard to do since the high bar was distance away from the bar she was already grasping onto. But she managed anyway and did it right. There were some cheers and clapping from the audience-that I'm guessing, uplifted her confidence-and did an excellent landing on her feet.

When she looked up' she was breathing heavily and was sweating a bit. She had a helper grab for her a towel and bottle of water. She then strode over to the bench and sat, not too close, next to Pirie. And then and on we had to wait for all the players to finish.

It has been about thirty minutes before both teams finished and believe me; the result was way too close to choose the winner. So with that happening, we had to wait another fifteen minutes before the mic went on and announced the winner, "And the winner of Fire Acrobats is, Zodda!" A huge ocean of cheers filled the arena and I could see Heather grin from ear to ear. It truly was a great win and you couldn't be happier. Just then, I realized that it was finally the time for Royal Archery. My heart pounded in my chest as Sr. Anders called our team to the opening. We didn't go just yet, since the field organizers of the tournament had to switch gear on the field so we could play.

As I was waiting, I looked up at the sky and saw that it was turning slightly dark. That was fine with me since I liked the dark more than the light. It has been something in my family for some time now, the fact that we all love the dark, is because a lot of my past relatives has come from the Dark Lands, a place that isn't too far from Kregilia. It's in our blood that we like the darkness. Mainly because our powers are lighting and thunder storms and that usually occurs at night. Most of my family members were the ones responsible for the rain and storms that is needed in Kregilia. My mother and father both done it before I was born, and soon I would too. But for now I was still too young and that duty will have to wait.

We were still waiting behind the arena, when I felt a slight tug of pain on my shoulders and looked sideways to see who did it. And when I did, my eyes immediately narrowed at who was standing there. It was none other than, my biggest rivalry, Paige Zires.

"Hey Kate," she said in a mocking way which did not make me happy, and I replied back sharply, "What do you want, Paige?" She chuckled and looked sideways before answering, "Oh nothing, really. Well, actually, yes. I do want to wish you luck. You will badly need it." My mind raced with dark thoughts at what to say back at her. Possibly darker than her hair that is. It was gelled backwards with a clumsy ponytail at the back.

I quickly erased all the dark thoughts and decided to say something else. I smirked wickedly and said, "Oh, well, thank you then Paige." As I was about to turn back, I also added, "Oh and by the way, I think *you* might need some luck on your hair. It looks awful." And with that I didn't dare look back to see her reaction and just went forward until I reached the field.

# ⚡ CHAPTER NINE ⚡

Royal Archery was bigger than I had expected it to be. This year, they surprisingly added more targets to shoot at and some extra ground so we had enough space. It was pleasant.

Zodda and Thorcle both lined up, but this time not on the field. Now the two teams stood against the far end wall and the players will be called upon individually. I was bit nervous about this idea but tried not to think about all the thousands of fans here, all eyeing on me. I wasn't much of a stage person and normally get shy and embarrassed fast. But this was sports and athleticism. And that is my thing so I mustn't be afraid.

The point of Royal Archery is to see how fast and how many targets you could hit in less than fifteen minutes. The more you get targets and finish in less than time, the more points you earn. I have done this once before, so it shouldn't be that difficult. But the only problem there is that this year you're being timed and that part was challenging. It was easier when you could hit freely, but since we we're all getting older and more skilled every second, they decided to harden it up. This was definitely going to be hard.

At the far end wall where we stood, the two teams huddle in their own small groups and were in deep conversations. I was standing around the middle of the circle and peered over to team Thorcle to see if I could spot Paige. Luckily I did, and as soon as I spotted her I turned my head away. Trying to give her the hint that I didn't care what she had to say and that I was brave about this whole event. I smiled shortly after, remembering when I gave her that insult earlier. I was in my thoughts but soon got back out as the sharp whistle blew and the first player went out.

She was from Thorcle. I could tell because the students in Thorcle wear slick and gleam outfits. All the time actually. While Zodda students wear bright and dark outfits. Bit the same but Thorcle students add extra shine or gel to mesmerize their looks.

The girl stood in the middle of the field and hovered for a few seconds before the whistle blew and she started. She quickly grabbed her bow and arrows from her back and started shooting immediately. I noticed that she brought out two arrows at the same time and was hitting very accurately. She didn't stutter nor hesitated to keep going. She went on for about twelve minutes until she hit all the targets that were floating in midair. Some were on the ground but mostly were floating. The student shot one more breathe and before heading off to get some water. A few minutes went on by and it was Thorcle's team to go again. The student that came out was Paige. I inhaled sharply and narrowed my eyes at her. She and I have been really close friends back then when we were little. We used to joke around all the time and play as if we were sisters. She used to tell me all the time that we were going to be best friends no matter what happened. Unfortunately, that was never true and when I achieved and successfully beaten her in a friendly competition in archery and got sponsored to ParceHollow before she did. Paige become a black soul and betrayed our friendship. I should have known that she was never trustworthy. Even though she is from Thorcle and I'm from Zodda, she was the nicest Thorcle student that I had ever met. I thought she would be like this forever but I was wrong. She is nothing more than a traitor. And from that day on, our rivalries and competitions started and would never end. We'll make sure of it.

As Paige got out on the field she swiftly took out her bow and arrows and when the whistle blew, she started. She was shooting like crazy. She went on without even stopping. She might have dropped a few arrows in the process, but it was worth the effort of winning Royal Archery. I saw that Paige only had three targets left but she was tired already. This was a disadvantage for her, of course. Although Paige was wearing out she didn't stop. At her last target she quickly first wiped off a sweat on her forehead and then aimed for it. It got hit and then the amount of time she took in Royal Archery was shown on a screen. Ten minutes. That was good. Too good. I gulped and tried to calm myself down as it was now my turn to play.

I slowly approached on the field and clenched my palm around my silver and black bow. It felt good to touch it. It remind me of the things it could do and the things I could do with it. I then slowly got out one arrow and looked over at the crowed. I noticed a lot of my relatives and surprisingly, my father. I smiled at the thought that he came to watch.

I waited a few more seconds until the whistle blew and I was off. I perfectly managed to shoot the first arrow and the next and so on. I got a target and another and another. I wasn't really aware of what seemed to go around me or how much time had passed. I was so fixed on this right now that I didn't even realize I was holding my bow or arrows. I just shot and shot with no worries whatsoever at this time. The only goal I had was to hit all the targets as fast as I could. I only had five targets left. Relieved, that only a few were left. It's not like I was tired or anything. I was very good at playing something for a long time without getting tired quickly. I could do this all day but it was just right now, kind of exhausting.

"There is one target to go," I thought. "Won't be so hard. I got this." I was sure I did. Before I turned right to hit the last target, I felt something hard go against my eyes. It felt like a very strong beam of light burning my eyes. It caused me to stumble back and I missed the shot. The crowd gasped at my unexpected stumble and grew silent. I groaned in pain as I rubbed my eyes. Clearly whatever it was, I couldn't see very well. I suddenly realized that the game was still on and time was ticking.

I tried my hardest to stand up but it was too difficult since the bright beam also kind of stunned my head and I was spinning. I shook my head firmly and squinted in search for my bow and arrows. Eventually I did and quickly placed an arrow in shooting position and aimed for the target that was a few feet away from me. As I did I suddenly tripped and fell on my hands, not sure where my arrow landed. There was commotion, silence, whispering, and gasp all coming from the audience. After a short second, the arena burst into roars of cheers. I had no idea what was going on and looked up to see my very own arrow stuck in the middle of the target.

# ⚡ CHAPTER TEN ⚡

The huge arena at ParceHollow Academy cheered, and it all seemed blurry at first but then soon came to vision.

I carefully stood up – still feeling the after math of the beam earlier – and smiled broadly. But my smile soon widened as I saw how much time it took for me. Eight minutes! I was beyond happy. I beat Paige by two minutes! I couldn't believe it actually happened, but it did and I was victorious. I blew a wave through the arena before walking over backstage of the academy. I had to, since I was technically *injured* and the medic, Ms. Selena, had to check on me.

She was a woman around her 20's that had long brown hair that was normally braided into the back. I knew her but not a lot. Since she was a doctor in training and only checks on minor issues, we don't see her often. She is a very quiet person and normally doesn't speak much. That was fine with me.

She led me into a short hallway and then into a small room on the left. When we walked in, she let me take a seat and started to work. "So, Kate do you know what happened earlier? Why you stumbled back?" Selena asked. I sighed and replied, "I don't know actually. I was just standing there and then, there it was. The beam of light hit on my eyes and caused me to fall." "Hmm." She thought for a moment before saying, "Okay. Wait here and give me a few seconds to get something. Here." She handed me a bottle of cold water and stood up to leave. I thirstily drank half of the water down. It felt nice going down my throat. It was feeling rather scratching.

A few minutes went by, before I heard a knock on the door. "Come in." I called. The door opened and instead of Selena, Heather stood in the doorway. "Hey, Kate. Mind if I come in?" Heather asked. "Sure. No problem," I said. She looked rather tired than happy and flopped down at a near chair. She sighed and rubbed the back of her neck.

"I know I'm not doing well, but what happened to you?" I asked. Heather shook her head and gave me a look that always made me laugh and said, "Oh, you have no idea how exhausting it was to do Fire Acrobats! It took every inch of my energy out of me." "I see. Makes sense at what you did out there," I commented. "Yea well, speaking of events, what happened to you? I mean you literally got caught off guard and missed your shot. You eventually got it later but still, something happened," Heather said. I shrugged and said, "Dunno. Maybe I got lost in focus and just acted stupid." "Or maybe that acting all belong to Paige," Heather stated. This captured my attention and asked, "What? What does Paige have anything to do with this? I mean she..." "She was cheating Kate," Heather said, cutting me off. I still looked confused and she explained, "Well, I'm not entirely sure what she did, but I saw her earlier today carrying around a small mirror." "Mirror?" I asked. "Well, something like that. She might have used it to shine it on your eyes when you or anybody else was looking." I looked at Heather for only a moment before punching my fist on my thigh. "Argh! That lying, stinking, cheating." "Calm down Kate. It's not that big of a deal. I mean you did beat Paige at her own Game, right? She failed in trying to fail you. You can rub it in her face afterwards!" Heather said trying to calm down me.

"You're right. I shouldn't think about it too much. And besides, you're right. I did bust up her plan, didn't I?" I said, smirking. "Yes you did!" Heather laughed and playfully punched me on my face.

We talked and I waited for Selena to return. She did and when she saw Heather, she cocked an eyebrow, "Um...is this your friend, Kate?" I nodded, "Yeah, can she stay?" Selena chuckled and smiled, "Of course she can." I smiled back and Heather made room for Selena to work on me.

She first dampened a cloth with warm water and gently applied it on my face. When was done with that, she then dried it off. "What did you do that for? I asked. "Oh, the beam may have burned your face a little too. There were some small red burnt areas so I just washed them away" Selena replied. I nodded. Selena then reached for what looked like a light stick and shined it on my eyes. I winced back, clearly not wanting any more pressure on my eyes than it already has. "It's oaky, Kate. This beam won't hurt you. I promise. This will just measure how strong your eye power is and we'll see how much you lost." I sighed and let her do it. It took only a second before Selena pulled back. She didn't look too satisfied. "What's wrong?" I asked. Selena sighed and said, "Nothing is wrong, Kate. It's just that you did lose some eye power. I thought it would be a small amount. Guess I was wrong. You have lost a great deal." I fumbled around with my hair and looked down. This was horrible news. I can't believe that Paige would, not only cheat, but cause me to lose some eyesight. I was so angry I could just—

"But there is a way to fix this" Selena broke. I looked up, "Really?" "Yes. We can apply artificial lenses on your eyes and they can help regain your eyesight." I frowned, "Will they be put on mandatorily?" "No, just until you gain your power back, they can be removed." I smiled in relief. I didn't want to have any artificial things on my face that would block out my natural eyes.

"When can I get them on?" I asked. Selena thought for a moment before replying, "We can do it today if you don't mind. A lot of injuries occurred today but they're all minor. We can get yours finished quickly." I smiled, "Thank you Selena." She smiled back, "Your welcome Kate." And with that, she left the room to book my appointment. So it was just Heather and I.

"So…Kate. Are you nervous about the whole contact lens thing?" Heather asked. "Nah, not really. I mean this is nothing compared to what I do every day," I said. "True," Heather agreed. "So what about Pirie?" I asked. "What about him?" Heather said worriedly. "Oh, nothing. It's just that his performance out there was pretty cool, eh?" I grinned. Heather shrugged, "I guess. Nothing too impressive really." "Uh-huh. Sure it wasn't", I said still teasing. Heather smiled and rolled her eyes, "Oh, quit it Kate. You're really not going to get anything through this conversation." I laughed and said, "Okay, okay. I'll stop. Just messing around with you. Gosh, you take things so seriously all the time." Now this caught Heather off guard and she threw a bottle of water at me. "Hey!" I squealed. Heather kept going and soon enough, if she doesn't stop, I'd be soaked all the way up to my socks. "Heather! Seriously, cut it out!" I yelled through laughs. She finally did and said, "You know, you're not the only one that can be silly at times."

# ⚡ CHAPTER ELEVEN ⚡

It has been almost an hour since I have left the hospital wing, feeling the urge of take off my contact lenses but I can't, which was unfortunate. Heather eventually went back to the locker rooms but I decided to see someone first. Someone that I've been dreading to see. And that someone was standing right across from me. I narrowed my eyes just at the sight of her and sighed. I really needed to make sure that Paige actually cheated during my performance. I do believe Heather but I needed to see if it was true.

So as I came up to her, I slightly pulled her shoulder back so she can face me. A second later I spilled out, "Nice going out there. You did a great job of not failing." Paige frowned and said, "Well I would have been happier if it wasn't for you." I cocked an eyebrow, "Speaking of me, how'd you like me out there? I was pretty cool right?" She grit her teeth slightly and then spat at the ground. Her attitude burned me with anger inside and I finally broke out, "Why were you trying to cheat to make me loose?" She just looked at me and then said, "I have no idea what you're talking about Kate." She was about to turn away but I pulled her shoulder back again and roughly said, "You know exactly what I'm talking about."

Paige again looked at me like I've lost my mind and said, "Well what if I did?" "Why" I asked. She made a sound of irritation and replied, "Because you're always number one! Always! I'm always left behind while you go on as the eye candy. And I'm sick of that!" I just stood there shocked and said, "I would've left you behind if I knew how you felt." "Well you did, and you can't change that," Paige grunted. I rolled my eyes in frustration and said again, "So were you the one that shone the light in my eyes?" Paige looked at the floor then shrugged carelessly, "I don't know." I balled my hands from exploding out anger and inhaled sharply, "I know you did it." "How would you know? You don't have any proof whatsoever," Paige said. I grinned, "I don't need proof. I can already tell you're a coward by your lazily personality."

This captured every bit of Paige's attention and with one sudden act; she was now standing inches away from my face. Through hate in her voice she spoke, "Don't you ever....say that again." "Or what," I challenged. Without words, Paige backed away and left out of my sight. "Pleasant," I thought of myself.

"You told her that she had a lazily personality?" My dad asked, astounded. I nodded, "Uh-huh." He chuckled and said, "Well we all have those moments, don't we? Blurting out nonsense words in such times." I grinned, "Well she deserved it. After all that she has put me through."

The tournament has recently ended and I was back home. Super exhausted, I slouched down on the coach. Since I didn't have anything to do, my dad decided to discuss with me about my issue. "So you're sure that you're feeling okay? I mean you had a mighty accident out there," my dad said. "Don't worry dad.

I'm okay. Everything fine except for my eyes," I said. He sighed, "It's nothing Kate, just some eyesight loss. You'll cure up soon." I nodded, "I hope so." After an hour of chatting, I quickly headed back up to my room where I collapsed on the bed, sighing heavily. Today was fun, it really was. Even with all the things that went by, I still had a good time today. And hopefully, moments like these would soon come back again. I know they will. They have to. Or what else could I have done.

With these thoughts buzzing my mind, I looked out at the pitch black sky that was filled with sharp silver stars. I smiled, remembering when my mom used to tell me stories about some travelers using the sky night as their only way to get out of danger. I still recall back these stories and amuse myself with them. The stories would always come back...but my mom never will.

I sighed; I really needed to stop thinking about these dark thoughts. But I can't stay away from them. When my mom passed away it's been giving me cold feelings since that day. I never really gotten over her death and probably never will, even though that situation happened way back. But I can't always look in the past. If I keep my ground and look ahead to what's coming, maybe I would stay more positive and not be so negative all the time. But it definitely will be hard for sure. It's kind of impossible to get over a tragic event that occurred in your life. So with that being said, I stood up in bed and walked over to my window, now getting a clear view of the moon and stars. It was very beautiful, possibly the most beautiful thing I have ever seen.

Suddenly I smiled, thinking of the great day I had at the tournament. I will never forget it. Being that close to losing and still winning is surely something not too common. But it happened anyway and I was dazed. To be honest, everyone at the game worked hard today, whether it was out opponents or friends. Such hard effort was put in. I honestly think that's a great way to start a terrific legacy. Silly as it was, I hope my legacy comes out smooth. I stared back up at the sky then at the ground. Entirely different but are still in the same world.

I thought about tomorrow and what possibly would be brought, many things of course. Every day is a new beginning of something that's already taking place.

# ⚡ CHAPTER TWELVE ⚡

It has been about a week since the Annual Tournament took place. Everyone was chirping about it at training so it was pretty much the topic to talk about for now.

It has also been a week ever since I got my contact lenses on too. They were very uneasy at first, but they're adjusting. Ms. Selena, the doctor who gave them to me, said to wash them daily in case any germs affect it. And so I do. It's a pretty hard job, but I will do anything to get my eyesight back. I just had to be patient, which is something I'm not too good at sometimes.

I grumbled and picked up another flying ball and tossed it in the air as hard as I could. But unfortunately, it didn't land far enough and I had to try again.

Today's training lesson was all about strength and how good we aim. Each one of us had to pick a heavy ball – I mean, *very* heavy – and try to through it as far as we could. All the students seem to be struggling at this. Even the strongest ones in the academy kind of had trouble throwing it properly. I tried one more time and if I didn't get it this time, I'm out. Lucky for me, it did go farther than my last shot but not far enough so flopped down on the ground and just sat there.

A few minutes passed away and my break time was over, so I stood up to train again. But before I could go and get a ball, I heard a voice behind me, "Pretty hard, huh? I can tell because you're sweating like crazy." Startled, I whipped around and saw that it was Siffrin. I narrowed by eyes and placed a hand on my chest, and said, "You should really stop doing that! You are going to give me a heart attack one day." Siffrin laughed and said, "Stop doing what?" "Stop scaring by just popping out of nowhere", I said. "Oh sorry," he said, still amused. As I was about to leave, I stopped and asked, "Wait, what you are doing here? I thought you already graduated from ParceHollow." Just as he was about to answer, I also added, "Also, why's your hair like that?" "Like what?" Siffrin asked. "Your hair......it's a different color," I said. "Oh, yeah, that. Um...I don't know actually. Every day it seems to be growing darker. I'm really not doing anything," he said while shrugging. I nodded and said, "Ok then. Oh, you haven't answered my first question. Why are you here exactly?" He brushed a hand along his, now kind of brownish hair, and said, "Why I am here. Good question. Um...well, I usually come here to train out my daily practice, but today I volunteered to help some classes." My eyes widened and I said, "Seriously? You're going to be teaching classes?"

"Well, technically not all classes, just a few here and there. You know, extra help if needed," he replied. I smiled and said, "Cool." He smiled back. I was about to turn back but at that moment, Heather bumped into me, making us both crush on the floor. I stood up first and shook my head, a bit dizzy from the collision,

"Woah Heather, watch where you're going, ok. What made you run like that?" She, too, was a little shaky and when that was over, she said, "Oops. Sorry there Kate. My partner accidently sent my ball flying towards your direction so I went after it. Unfortunately, I didn't notice you at all and bumped into you. I'm sorry again." I smiled and helped her up. When Heather stood up she not only eyed me, but the guy in front of her as well.

"Hey, who's this?" She asked. "Oh that's Siffrin. He's an um...well I guess you could call he's a friend of mine," I said, not sure whether we were. We met not too long ago, but it looked like we pretty much had a decent friendship. "Nice to meet you, Siffrin," Heather grinned. "Nice to meet you too, Heather," he replied back. A moment or two later, Heather spoke up, "Um, well I'll see you later Kate and you too Siffrin." "Where are you going?" I asked. She sighed, "Detention." At first, I stood there shocked but soon after, burst out laughing. "Detention, what in the world did you do Goody Girl?" Heather rolled her eyes and said, "I told you not to call me that. And I didn't do anything. I'm just going to help clean up around the place, that's all." I got myself together and said a little breathlessly, "Oh good. Because for a moment right there, I actually thought you did something bad. Wouldn't that be tragic for Ms. Goody Two Shoes here, now would it?" Since Heather was a month or two older than me, she simply just brushed it off and walked on. My laugh quickly faded and I called after her, "Oh come on, Heather. I'm sorry. I didn't mean to-Ah, never mind. She'll get over it."

I realized Siffrin was still standing there and I brushed a little at what he commented, "Wow, you two have a really unique relationship, don't you?" I shrugged and said, "Yeah, well that's how we really are every day, nothing new." "I see. I used to have a friend like that too, back in the day. We were pretty tight. But I don't know where he is now." "Oh? I questioned. "We don't really keep in touch anymore. He may have forgotten me. There was some silence after this and few minutes later, Siffrin spoke, awkwardly, "Well, I guess I've got to get going then. Surely the teachers must be waiting by now." "Yeah, you should go. I've got to head back to my training too." With a final last goodbye, we both went on our separate ways.

I only had one more class to go and then I would be done for the evening. My class that I'd be going to will be about how to cast invisible vortex objects such as; pots, cups, chairs, and more. It would be exciting, wouldn't it? I'll just have to see to find out. When the time came for the casting class, the field cleared out all the equipment from last class, and changed it into this current one. There were two long tables on each side of the arena that was filled with different potions dust. Each pot contains a different color for different spells. I honestly was little bit confused at this, but soon will get these answers solved eventually.

My mood brightened a little, once I saw that Heather was in this class too. She waved at me and I waved back. But she quickly turned her focus back to the person she was talking to. As I come closer, I noticed that it was Pirie and raised an eyebrow. But my thought was soon answered when I walked up to them and asked, "Hey guys, what's up?" "Oh, nothing, Pirie and I were assigned as partners so we're just discussing about the lesson we just got from the teacher, Sr. Jacobs," Heather replied then passed me a sheet of paper that was filled with spells they had to do. There were at least 20 of them here. I looked up and asked Pirie, "I didn't know you take potions." "Well, I do but not on a basic ritual. I normally do it time-to-time," he answered. Before we could continue any further, a voice called out, "Alright students, get in position please." We all lined up in a clumsy line but that didn't really matter. Sr. Jacobs spoke, "Good evening every one. Now as you all know you have been passed a paper that includes all the spells you will be doing today. Now I know you are all thinking that there is too much to do, so I brought in, an assistant that will help you doing the way." "Who was the assistant," I thought. There was some commotion and then it was followed by cheers and happy greetings. I looked through the crowed to see who it was, and it was, surprisingly, Siffrin who was standing there.

# ⚡ CHAPTER THIRTEEN ⚡

Siffrin smiled at every one and jogged over to meet them. They all hugged, high-fived, and all spoked to him at the same time. They were all glad that he was back.

"Hey every one, nice to see you guys again! I really missed training here every day with all of you. But hey, I'm here now aren't I?" Siffrin stated. Some of the students laughed a bit. Then I saw Pirie walk up to him, and gave him a playful smack on the back of Siffrin's head. "Wow, same old Siffrin eh…you haven't changed one bit since the last time I saw you," Pirie said. Siffrin shrugged and said, "Well, I guess I'm just lucky I haven't been different. You know some people do change quickly. People like….you." "Yeah right," Pirie chuckled then pulled Siffrin in a tight, quick hug. "Alright everybody, now that you all have greeted your old dear friend, I suggest we get to work now, hmm?" Sr. Jacobs said. We nodded and began training.

Every pair of partners went out to the two tables and started to cast. I noticed I didn't have a partner, and went up to Sr. Jacobs. "Um, excuse me sir. I don't really have someone to work with." Sr. Jacobs raised his eyebrows in shock and said, "Oh, I haven't given you one? But you have your paper, right?" I nodded. "Okay then. Um…, I guess you go work with any pair you want; it's your choice, Kate." I thanked Sr. Jacobs and then headed out to pick out a group.

Since I was familiar with Heather and Pirie, I decided to go there. As I walked over to them, they both exclaimed: "We need your help!" I laughed and said, "Woah, okay. Sure. What's the problem?" "Your mother has come from part of the Divinition Valley, right? You kind of know about how to use potions, so can you help us out? I mean, you do know some, don't you?" Heather asked. "Oh, yeah sure. I can help you guys out. What do you need help on?" I replied. Heather shoved the paper in my face, and teasingly said, "The whole thing obviously." I giggled and looked at the first spell we had to do. "Alright, this potion needs blue dust, green dust, and orange dust for the mix. Have we got any?" I said.

"Yeah, I think we do. Here, let me go grab them," Pirie said. When he came back from the other table, he was holding all three bottles of dust. He set them down on the table and then asked, "Okay...now what?" I looked around the table and noticed a medium sized bowl that everyone was using, so I went to get one as well. "May be we can mix the potions in this. It's big enough to make in," I said, setting it down. "You're right, let's get started," Pirie said.

After a few minutes of adding in the mixtures, we were finally done. It looked like a dark mix of color, but that didn't matter. What mattered was on how it worked and tasted to the person, who was going to drink it, then cast it with their hands. "So, who want to go first?" Heather asked. I shrugged and volunteered to go, "Oh whatever. I'll do it. We put everything together accurately, it'll be fine." "I don't know, Kate. It doesn't really look right to me. Look, we got the end color wrong. We were supposed to get a light and dull mixture, but instead we got a dark one," Pirie stated.

I sighed and said, "Well, there's only one way to find out for sure and that's by drinking it." I carefully lifted the bowl and gulped down a small portion of the mixture. I shivered, it didn't taste that good either. I was worried a little about this but there was no going back now. I exhaled slowly and raised my hands in front of me to start the spell. I began to feel a little bit of spark float between my fingers and palm. I kept going until there was a fully matured spark ball in my hand. But suddenly, it began to burn a little. Then again and again it began to heat up my entire hand. I gasped and frail my hands to get rid of it, but then realized I accidently sent it flying in Siffrin's direction.

"Oh, no, this isn't good! What gone wrong? Why didn't it--," I started saying before stopping at the sight of the spark ball reaching in further towards Siffrin. "Siffrin look out!" I shouted. Siffrin immediately whipped around and, just by the second managed to prevent the ball to hit him. I stood there for a moment, Siffrin walked over to us and smiled, "Having a hard time here, aren't we?" I sighed and replied "You bet. This thing is impossible to do." Siffrin chuckled and said, "Well, you'll get better with some practice. No need to be ashamed. Even when I first started, I was the biggest failure in my class." Pirie snorted and said, "Yeah you were." Siffrin stuck his tongue out at Pirie, which made him snicker harder.

"Speaking of your powers, how did you manage to block out that ball so quickly? I could've sworn it nearly hit you." "Oh, it's a special gift of mine. For all my family members really; my mom, dad, and sister. We all can detect a spell when it will come near us or so. By seeing and sensing the spells earlier, it makes it easy for us to cast." I understood then said, "Wait, you have a sister?" Siffrin smiled and said, "Yeah. Her name is Mable and she came into ParceHollow not too long ago. About 8 months she has been here. She is now 12 years old." "Oh, so was that the girl that entered Extreme Medivial and nearly got thrown off. I'd reckon she'd be your sister. You guys share a lot of similarities." "I know, many people say that," he said smiling. "So...what are we going to do now?" Heather asked awkwardly. "Oh, we could continue our tasks in making spells. We've still got a lot more to do and more practice since the last one completely backfired," Pirie said. "Yeah, we should get started on these other spells too. We barely have enough time left," I said. "Hey why don't I work with you guys? You could use some help here and there. By the looks of it, you could set a student on fire," Siffrin joked. "Oh, shut up Siffrin," I said, clearly embarrassed at what I did earlier. But that didn't help out too much, now that Siffrin, Pirie, and Heather all laughed their heads off. I sighed and rolled my eyes. Nice friends.

It was almost night time and at last, all the groups have finished with their spells. To be honest, I thought everybody is extremely tired. I could tell because they were all drooping and falling on one another so they don't pass out because they drank way too many mixtures. Even I was super exhausted and couldn't wait to go home and sleep on my nice, cozy bed. I could tell Heather and Pirie wanted to do the same. Siffrin didn't look as much tired, mainly because he just helped us and didn't try any mixtures – which were all pretty bad-, and helped us walk out of the training arena. I remembered that I had a personal training lesson with Coach Bozz tomorrow morning, and quickly waved everyone goodbye so I can get an early start on class tomorrow.

# ⚡ CHAPTER FOURTEEN ⚡

"Again," Coach Bozz commented on my failed routine. It had to be early dawn by now and I made sure to come to the academy as early as possible.

I heavily breathed in and out, while wiping a sweat that was triggering down forehead. I was very furious about my not-so-good- performance but was trying to hide it from Bozz. I didn't want to let him see that I was mad already. He'd think that I couldn't do the job right and gave up only because I didn't want to try again. So I exhaled out and picked the stuff that I was using and tried again to do the Black Dragon. It needed loads of power from the person that was doing it, and it sure as ever drained out my power from my body. It was a highly advanced martial arts move that only few know to succeed. Bozz wanted to teach me this since I was the only student in the entire academy that had the most stability – for all that I know. He was positive that I could master it in time, but it didn't look like that was going to happen.

I tried again and failed again. I scowled, I don't know how in the world that I managed to win Royal Archery at the grandest game of all in Kregilia's history, and not be able to achieve at a simple move like the Black Dragon in an ordinary looking arena with nothing but my sweatshirt and black jeans. And at that thought, a nerve of mine had finally cracked and screamed out-loud, throwing away the stuff. Just then I realized that I had started weeping a little and Bozz laid a hand on my shoulder to sooth me down. "Breathe, Kate. It's not that big of a deal that you can't strive in this move. I just wanted to test to see if you could do it or not. And-," Coach Bozz was saying before I cut him off, yelling at the top of my lungs, "You don't think I care! I most certainly do! I want to achieve my goals, I want to win! Coach, all I want is to pass my tests. But that's never going to happen." He sighed and started again, but I spoke over first, "Don't you see that I am failing? I am not like the others in the academy. Everyone, I mean everyone, is succeeding and leaving. Even Heather! Even she is in top league. Coach Bozz, I don't want to be the only one left here...I need help."

He stared at me and I stared at him right back. I hadn't noticed but that's what we actually did the entire time. I was hardly aware on how long we stayed like this but I honestly didn't care. I just wanted to hear Bozz's words coming out of his own mouth at what he thought of my outburst. But the only thing that he did was smile. Smile? How can he be amused at this very tense moment here? He saw the confused look on my face and answered my question, "Have you been thinking about it?" "Thinking about what?" I asked, calmly this time. "About going to your new training academy, have you thought over it?" Bozz said. I sighed and replied, "Well, I mean I have been thinking about it lately, but I hadn't made up my mind yet." Bozz thought for some time before asking another question, "Why? Why haven't you made up your mind yet?" "I don't know. I guess I'm still hooked over the fact that I'm going to be leaving my father and my friends, and—" I was saying before Bozz cut me off,

"See right there. That's the problem why you can't focus on your training. You're scared and worried about leaving your close ones behind, Kate. That's why you're not moving quickly enough." "Yes, but how would you know—""Because I've seen the way you work, Kate. You like to be close with the ones you love and care about. Now tell me if I'm wrong or right, but I thought you were different from the others. Remember you said that?" "Well, yes," I said somberly. "But if you want to step up your game Kate, then you're going to have to, just a little, push away your feelings forward your family and friends."

"So what are you saying Coach?" I asked. "You're too kind, Kate. You need to step up, and look deeper in your training and powers. You are also too soft. Push your highest limits and don't ever stop, ok? Everyone can shoot up towards their limits and break it. You're just holding them back," Coach Bozz said in a nice and short talk. This all made sense now, I thought. May be this is why I was falling behind. I need to become more aggressive and break through my limits that are holding me back. But will I ever do that?

"But Coach, how can I become stronger in my power? How can I do them? Who will help me?" I said. I might have seen something flash in his dark eyes before he answered, "Demons Cave Academy." "Demons what now?" I asked, confused. "Demons Cave Academy, it's a highly structured training ground that's located at Flourin, our neighbor country. It's a very much classified academy where I'm sure you will learn a lot there...well, if you actually went." I blinked in surprise and thought it over. That academy does sound hardcore and that's exactly what I need to overcome my weakness, and better yet, be way more skilled at my powers. May be this IS exactly what I needed the entire time. I need – No, have to go to DemonsCave. It will be perfect and, and – wait. Do I really want to go? Well I don't feel like going. But I have to. Coach Bozz has recommended this academy to help me, because he knew exactly what I needed. But what if he doesn't? What if I don't make it out at where I'm going? Will I ever make a good impression of myself?

All of these questions buzzed through my mind. A part of me wanted to stay firmly where I am, but the other part wanted to go there so badly and so eager that it could just go right now if it could. I inhaled a shaky breathe and looked down at my hands. They were bit red from all the blood that was pumping around inside of them. I know, and everybody knew that this would be the best for me and that it will do me good. Hesitance, that's what I was suffering from right now. I didn't know either to say yes or no. I closed my eyes and cleared out my mind tried to focus. Oh man, please let me. I thought very hard and so deeply that I wasn't even aware that my eyes were a bit teary since I shut my eyes so hard and for so long. I had made up my answer.

"Yes. Yes, I will go to DemonsCave Academy and try my hardest to accomplish something there," I said, trying to hold ground. Coach Bozz sighed and nodded his head in approval. I breathed out. I could not believe that I actually made that decision. I prayed that I had made the right one.

# N CHAPTER FIFTEEN N

I slurped down the hot sizzling tea that was brewing in my mug as I looked out the window watching the birds chirp away in their own little world.

I sometimes wondered what it would be like if I weren't a human. I wondered if I was just a free wild animal that could do whatever I wanted with no care in the world. That would've been awesome, I can assure you that much. You know, just to roam around the lands of forbidden, to do illegal things without anyone knowing, or even just to sit there in your own space and do nothing at all. No worries, no tension. Nothing would ever bug you.

I thought of these peculiar things just when I heard a knock on the door. I set the mug down and walked up to the door to see who it was. Luckily it was only Heather so I let her in. "Hey Kate. Mind if I crash at your place? I got nothing going on right now," Heather said coming in. I shrugged, "Yeah sure, why not? I don't have any plan either." We laughed a little before sitting down on the table.

Heather peeked through my mug and asked, "What are you drinking, hot tea?" I nodded, "Only the best. It was shipped from DiLa Crunel." Heather sighed, "DiLa Crunel. Oh how I wish I could go there. They are such a fancy city that makes the most wonderful treats." "Can they also re-make your odd face into a treat?" I grinned. "Blah, blah, blah" Heather mocked, rolling her eyes. "Anyway, how'd your training go yesterday with Bozz?" Heather asked. I stopped drinking and sighed, "That's what I wanted to talk to you about." Heather put on a puzzled face and said, "What's up? You can tell me anything." "Well," I started, "Yesterday while I was training with Bozz, we talked...talked about a lot of.....things." "Things like what?" Heather asked. I first looked around the place before telling her everything, "Over the past month, Bozz and I have been discussing certain things about me and my training. You already know that I'm not too good at my powers unlike everyone else, so Bozz urged me transferring into a new training academy."

Heather's eyes went big and asked, "Move to another academy? Well where is it? When will you be going?" I shrugged and replied, "I dunno when I'm going but for all that I heard so far is that the new academy is called DemonsCave and it's located at Flourin." Heather went quiet for a few moments before speaking up, "And what did you say as your answer, Yes or no?" I bite the inside of my cheek and shook my head, "I'm sorry Heath. I had to say yes. It's what the best for me. I honestly didn't think that I'd be agreeing but I did. And there is not going back now." "Why not, why can't you go back?" Heather said, eyeing me. I took another sip of my now not-so-hot tea anymore before answering, "Because it is what it is, ok. Look I know you're mad." "Why would I be mad at you for going into the greatest academy in the world?" Heather broke me off saying. I raised an eyebrow, "Greatest academy in the world?" Heather nodded, "Yep. My older brother was raised in Flourin before I was born and got enrolled at DemonsCave." "He did?" I asked. "Uh-huh.

He started hard at first but soon after came out with ease before fully graduating. My parents were gonna send me there as well, but that was the year Kregilia had its war and every country happened to just, you know stop functioning for a while," Heather ended. It took me time to sink this in until I said, "I see. So you're not mad at me?" "Not at all Kate, I think you should go, you know it's for the better good," Heather said smiling. I smiled back.

Sighing, I finished the last of me tea when Heather asked, "By the way, how is your father doing Kate?" "Oh he is doing well..., I guess. I might send him to Kregilia's Hospital," I answered. Heather scrunched of her nose and said, "Why would you want to send him there?" I shrugged, "Bozz says that's the best for now, but I'll think it over later." "Ok, cool. Uh, I guess I should get going. I mean, you will be busy later, you know," Heather stated. "Yah, I guess you are right," I said. We stood up from our chair and I led her to the front door. We said our goodbyes and I closed the door and walked up to my room.

"Wait, you're leaving?" Siffrin asked eyeing me. Siffrin, Pirie, and I were outside a local café that was pretty close to the academy. It was by noon now and I decided to tell Siffrin and Pirie about my farewell. And by the way things were going they weren't too happy about it.

"Yeah... I am," I answered him. He lean back on the table, looking down at the concrete ground. I sighed quietly. Pirie looked at me and smiled, "Don't worry Kate. It'll be ok. You just have to wait and see what will happen next. And the only way that you're gonna be able to do that is by trying it out. You'll see trying new things isn't a bad thing." I smiled sweetly at him and he continued, "Even when I tried to become a new friend of Siffrin, I thought I was going to screw up, judging that horrible face of his when he gets mad." Pirie and I laughed out hard and Siffrin rolled his eyes, "I do not have a horrible face when I get mad." Pirie chuckled, "Yeah you do." I giggled some more and Siffrin shoot his head, but I knew he was smiling.

A few minutes past and Pirie soon had to leave. "Sorry guys can't stay any longer. I got some work that need to be finished. See you guys," Pirie said standing up to leave. I waved him goodbye and so did Siffrin before it was just the two of us now. He awkwardly laughed and said, "So, want dessert?" I shook my head, "No thank you. I already reached my limits." He smiled and spoke up later, "Want to go outside the café?" "Sure," I said. We went outdoors in the brisk sun and stood by the sidewalk, watching cars and trucks go by. "You know I'm going to miss you guys, right?" I said. Siffrin's lips twisted into a grin and he glanced sideways at me and said, "That's not a surprise at all... because we're all going to miss you too."

# ⚡ CHAPTER SIXTEEN ⚡

I brushed a hand along my hair and hopes that it will stay in place as I am going to encounter on a bumpy ride.

It was very early in the morning and I had just finished the last of my breakfast and took a shower. I had a delicious start on soothing wash but for some reason, I didn't feel any of it. I guess it was just the thought of me leaving Kregilia, but worse, I was leaving right now. I sighed and tried to contain myself from not spilling out sobs. I was really going to miss my home, my father, and specially my friends. But there was no chance of redeeming myself now. I have already got in fully ready and packed my things. I blink and looked around my room one final time. Why did it feel so empty? I don't know when it got like that but I know why. I rolled my head on my neck a couple of times before walking out the door, holding my bow and arrow in one hand and my bag in the other. I trotted down the stairs and noticed my father was standing by the door. I slowly walked up to him and smiled. He smiled back warmly and glanced towards my sudden appearance. "Well it looks you're ready," he spoke. I nodded, can't seem to find my voice. He sighed and caressed my face before hugging me. I embraced him back tight and then pulled away. "Good luck Katelyn. I know you'll do just fine," my dad said.

I bit the inside of my mouth from my great sorrow and nodded obediently. And with one last look towards Andrew Strike, I left the house, feeling confident as ever. Since the academy wasn't too far from my house, I walked the entire time, recalling my family's greatest memories. Some were fun and joyful and some were devastating and sad that caused me to walk faster.

I eventually made it to the academy just in time to find Bozz, Heather, Siffrin, Pirie, and all my other teachers waiting for me inside. I swallowed a lump that in my throat and walked up to them, eying each and every one of them with different thoughts going through my mind as I did. Bozz was the first one to walk up to me and gave me a welcoming hug. He pulled back and whispered, "Make me proud, Rookie." I silently laughed and then received hugs from all my teachers.

After I had finished my farewell with all of my masters, I then looked forward to greet Heather, who was already red eyed. I giggled and gasped for air as she gave me a bone crushing hug. When we pulled back she smiled but then sobbed again. I assured her by giving her one last hug and she seemed to have calmed down, but just a little. Next person I saw myself face to face was Pirie. I smiled as he offered me to hug him. "Have a great time over there," he said as we parted. "I'll make sure to," I grinned. And finally there was Siffrin. I rolled my eyes and presented him with a hug too. I pulled away and gradually punched him in the chest and then turned away, leaving him clueless.

I headed back over to Bozz and nodded, "I'm ready." Bozz grinned and said, "I know you are." After that, Bozz circled light blue and orange energy around his palms before showing it in the midfield. It created a large vortex entrance which will probably lead to DemonsCave. Bozz looked at me and said, "Don't worry, I've contacted one of my friends at Flourin to help you, so when you reach the other side, there will be someone waiting." I nodded surely before staring once again at the portal. What will await me there? Will I be able to make it through? When will I be back in time? Questions, just questions rang in the back of my head as I thought of DemonsCave and its new style. Boy was I nervous.

With one final glance towards my loveable teachers and dearest companions, I sighed heavily. I really wanted to make my father proud, but the only way to do that was to go through my greatest challenge. Well, it could be good, or it could be bad. Who knows, maybe both. Maybe Pirie was right, the only way I'd know for sure was to wait and see. After all, I may like it.

So with determination and fear boiling in my heart, I stepped into the gateway of my new world, with each step a new journey began, one that I couldn't wait for. I grinned, ready for anything that came by way. Believe it!

--End---

# ACKNOWLEDGEMENT

I wanted to write this book for fun and my love for writing. However I would like to give credit to my teachers who kept on compelling me to write more, especially my 4th grade teacher, Mrs. Howayda, who has always loved my work and wanted more of it. And So I shared my stories with her. Similarly, I gratefully acknowledge Mrs. Moeller (my 5th grade teacher), who was very excited to read part of this story (under development) and seriously encouraged for getting it published.

Also throughout my school life thus far, many of my friends have been entertained by my humor and said you should write it all down.

I am happy to admit that my younger sister, Lashirah who is 8 years old, often enthusiastically helped this work by typing on computer or by assisting in other ways. Gracious regards to my father, Dr. Lokman Hossain, who patiently read my writing in journal again and again with affection and supported the whole project from very beginning.

Above all, I am thankful to Almighty for His endless blessing and mercy that made it possible to accomplish this.

# ABOUT THE AUTHOR

**Saramah Hossain**

Saramah was born in 2005. She grew-up in Calgary City, Canada. She started her elementary school in Canada and completed up to 3rd grade. After that, she moved to Texas with her family and resumed from 4th grade and continued. She won numerous academic awards like the Principal's Award, Excellency Award and also received Honor Rolls.

Saramah finished this story as a 5th grader. She just turned to a 6th grader last week. Her first attempt to put together some words and making full sentences happened to be when she was a kindergarten student. One day during an instant writing lesson, she was able to write a page-long story where she tried to share her feelings about one of our family trips. The KG teacher showed us that story, when we had a parent-teacher meeting some days later, and asked, "Did you teach her anything about this story?" We replied, "No." That was the moment when we comprehended how much she loves to write. Since then, she has been encouraged by all of her class-teachers of different grades in different schools that she attended so far. One of her recent notable achievements occurred in 2015. She participated in the "Writing Contest" organized by the PSIA (Private Schools Interscholastic Association) and earned a place for her school.

This small piece of work is her very first original endeavor for a chapter book. Saramah currently lives in Texas, USA with her parents and younger sister.

*- From the parents' note (8/28/16)*

Printed in the United States
By Bookmasters